The
PIRATE
Cook
Book

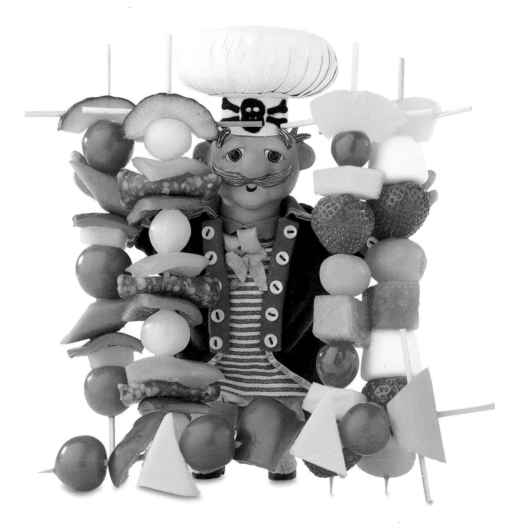

LONDON, NEW YORK, MELBOURNE,
MUNICH, and DELHI

Text by Mary Ling
Deputy Managing Art Editor Jane Horne
Editors Rachel Wardley and Carrie Love
Designers Karen Lieberman
and Gemma Fletcher
Jacket Editor Mariza O'Keeffe
DTP Designers Nicola Studdart
and Ben Hung
Home Economist Emma Patmore
Consultants Naomi Harrison
and Harry Sullivan
Pirate Pete conceived by Wilf Woods
Photography Dave King
Production Kate Oliver and Angela Graef

First American Edition, 1997
This edition published in 2007 by
DK Publishing
375 Hudson Street
New York, New York 10014

07 08 09 10 11 9 8 7 6 5 4 3 2 1

A catalog record for this book is available
from the Library of Congress.

ISBN: 978-0-7894-1519-6 (hardcover)
ISBN: 978-0-7566-3000-3 (paperback)
KC060 – 01/07

Color reproduction by Colourscan,
Singapore
Printed and bound in Italy by L.E.G.O.

Discover more at
www.dk.com

Contents

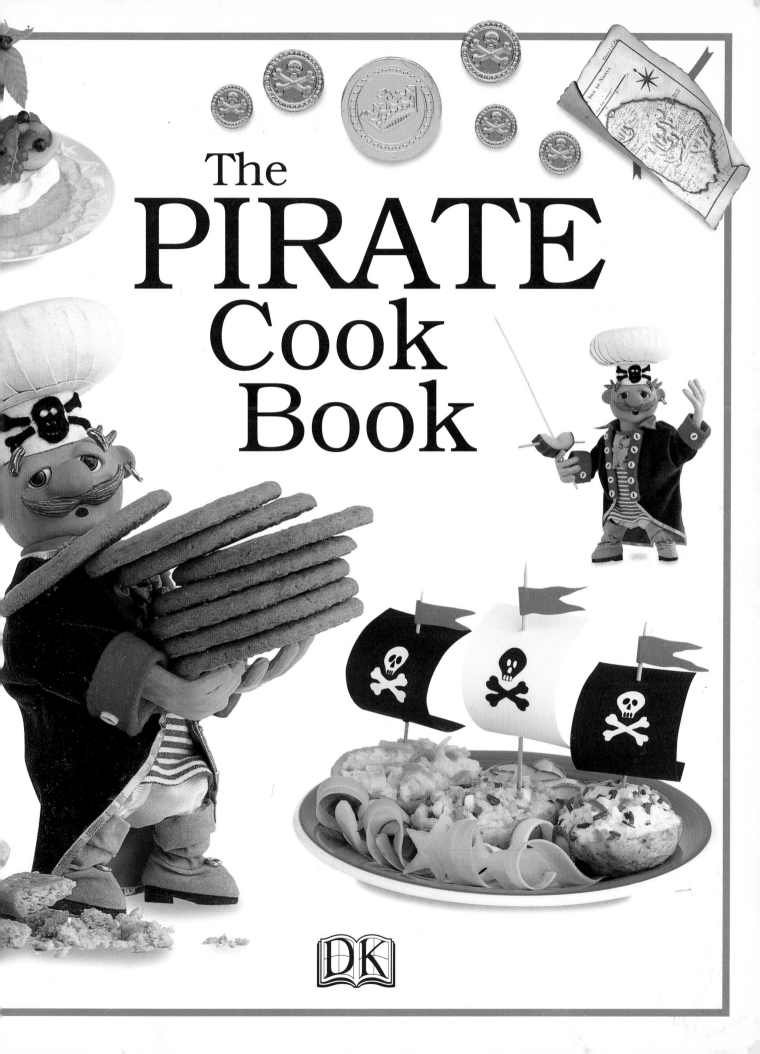

The
PIRATE
Cook
Book

DK

Galley Rules

1.  When the Jolly Roger is at full mast, an adult must be with you.

2. When the anchor is down, try some of your own ideas and ingredients.

3. Each recipe serves about four members of your crew.

4. Wash your hands before you start.

5. Wear an apron.

6. Collect all the ingredients you will need.

7. Be careful with sharp knives, and always use a cutting board.

8. Wipe up spills and clean up as you work. Keep the decks clear.

9. Turn saucepan handles to the side so that you don't bump them.

10. Use an oven mitt to hold hot things.

Cooks' Tools

knife

fork

spoon

cutting board

wooden spoon

bowls

muffin tin

whisk

grater

frozen bar molds

cookie sheet

blender

cookie cutters

pitcher

Techniques

Chopping

Place the food on a cutting board. Use a sharp knife to make downward cuts.

Grating

Hold the grater firmly and rub the cheese downward against the grater. Keep your fingers out of the way.

Skewering

Skewer a chunk of food by pushing a wooden skewer through its middle.

Mixing

Put the ingredients in a bowl and stir them together with a large spoon.

Whisking

Whisk egg whites by beating them quickly with a whisk until they are stiff and stand up in peaks.

Melting

Melt chocolate by putting it in a bowl over very hot water until it is liquid.

Crushing

To crush crackers, put them in a plastic bag and beat them with a rolling pin.

Blending

Use an electric blender or food processor to mix ingredients together well. Make sure that the lid is firmly closed.

Pirate Potato Boats

Jangling jellyfish! These'll warm your cockles

You will need 4 potatoes 3 tbs 45g } tuna   1 tablespoon mayo

2 tbs 30g } cooked corn  3 chopped scallions  cheese

1. Before you start, set the oven to 400°F/200°C.

2. Wash the potatoes, then pr**i**c**k** them with a fork. Wrap them in foil and p**o**p them in the oven.

3.  When the potatoes are soft, ask an old sea-dog to help you c**u**t them in half.

4. Chop and **grate** the ingredients for the fillings.

5. Spoon the inside of each potato into a bowl and mix with one of the fillings.

6. Then drop each mix back into a potato skin.

⚓ Invent some fillings of your own.

7. Set sail on a feast of filled boats **bobbing** on a sea of salad waves.

Cut-Throat Kebabs
A sweet and savory suprise on a stick.

You will need cheese a selection of your favorite fruits

and vegetables  cold cuts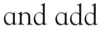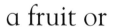

1. chop all the ingredients

into bite-sized chunks.

2. Take two

wooden skewers

and add

a fruit or

vegetable chunk to

make a

sword just like mine.

3. Then pick and **m^{i}x** as you thread

a selection of sweet and savory treats.  Be **c^{ar}ef$_{ul}$** not

to stab your finger while you are

doing it. Cut off

the ends of

the skewers.

4. Then they

are ready for the

hu^{n}gr$_{y}$

crew to eat. Just

make sure you

get some, too.

Desert Island Dessert

For shipwrecked sailors with a sweet tooth

You will need 2 egg whites   ½ cup 115g } sugar  gelatin

whipped cream chocolate sticks  lots of fruit

mint leaves

1. Before you start, set your oven to 250°F/120°C.

2. Pop the egg whites into a bowl and whisk them until they stand up stiff, like white horses on top of stormy waves.

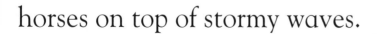

3. Sprinkle in sugar, little by little, while still whizzing your whisk.

4. Plonk blobs of the mixture onto a cookie sheet, making a well in the middle of each. **Bake** for about two hours.

5. Place the baked meringues on a sea of green gelatin and **pack** a raft with fruit.

6. No desert island is complete without palm trees made of chocolate trunks and mint leaf fronds in a **blob** of cream.

Booty Bundles
Dig in to a sea-time treasure trove.

You will need ^{4oz}/_{115g} } semi-sweet chocolate ^{1 cup}/_{250g} } butter

^{8 large}/_{60g} } graham crackers  2 tablespoons heavy cream

^{¼ cup}/_{55g} } candied cherries ^{¼ cup}/_{55g} } flaked almonds

^{1 tbsp}/_{15g} } raisins

1. **Crush** the crackers into tiny pieces.

Chop the cherries and mix them

with the nuts, raisins, and crackers.

2.  Ask an

ancient mariner to help you

melt

the butter, cream, and chocolate

together over very hot water.

3. **Mix** the melted chocolate with the cracker crumbs.

4. **Line** muffin tin cups with foil.

5. **Dollop** spoonfuls of mixture into the cups and pop the tin in the fridge.

6. **When** the mixture is as cool as an iceberg, **Scrunch** the foil and tie it with string. Your friends will think they've found treasure!

Titanic Treats
Let's sink a few of these jiggling icebergs.

You will need orange juice lime juice  melons

1. Press out sea creature shapes from the melon using nautical cookie cutters.

2. Lay the fruit shapes in frozen bar molds and then **fill** the molds with juice.

3. Be careful not to spill them as you pop them in the freezer until firm. **4.** Hold them upside down under running water 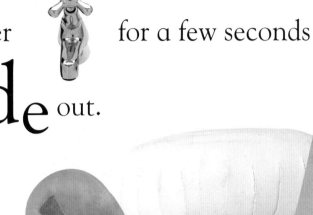 for a few seconds and they will slide out.

 Try other flavors of juice and different fruits for lots more titanic treats.

Tropical Tastes

These two juicy drinks shiver me shakes!

Milk shake: 1 scoop ice cream ⅔ cup 150ml } milk  6 large strawberries

Punch: ⅔ cup 150ml } cranberry juice  ⅔ cup 150ml } orange juice

1 orange 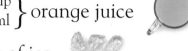 1 apple lots of ice

1. Wash 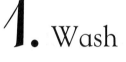 and **slice**

some plump, ripe

strawberries.

2. Plop all the ingredients

into a blender. **3.** Get

an old sea-dog to screw the lid on tight

and **whoosh** it all around until

everything is blended.

1. Take orange juice and cranberry juice, **pour** them into a pitcher, and stir. **2.** Cut the orange and apple into slices. **Pop** the slices and some ice cubes into the juice, too. ⚓ Serve these thirst quenchers to the crew with straws and extra fruit.

Shipmates' Snacks

It's a party! We'll have a whale of a time.

Fish snack: bread   tuna   mayo   pepper

cucumber   radish   olive

Nautical nibbles: bread   cheese and ham   olive

lettuce   soft cheese   pepper

1. s**l**i**c**e the

bread in half. To make a fish

shape, cut out two triangles

for a tail and one for a

mouth.

2. sp**r**e**ad** tuna

mixed with mayonnaise all over

the fish-shaped bread.

3. Thinly s^lice the pepper and arrange cucumber and radish slices on top to look like fish scales. Make an olive eye and pepper fins.

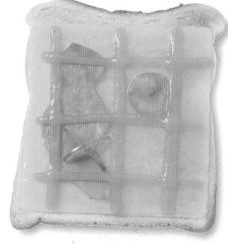

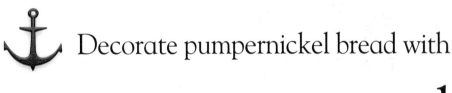 Decorate pumpernickel bread with a skull and crossbones squeezed from a tube of soft cheese.

 Grill a cheesy map on a piece of brown bread.

 Just copy this picture for a fine example of nautical nibbles.

Dive - in Dips

Fine food for hungry sailors.

Pirate peppers: 3 peppers ¹/₂ cup 115g } hummus paprika

Dig-in dips: corn chips  ¹/₂ cup 115g } guacamole 1 tomato

¹/₂ cup 115g } sour cream 1 avocado

Cannonball tomatoes: lots of cherry tomatoes 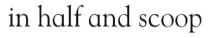 soft cheese

1. Chop some peppers

in half and scoop

out the seeds.

2. Fill

the pepper halves to the

brim with hummus. **3.** Make

a stencil to mark an

X of paprika.

1. **Fill** a bowl with guacamole and another with sour cream. Arm the crew with corn chips.

2. **Load** your corn chips until they overflow with diced tomato and avocado.

1. **slice** the tops off cherry tomatoes.

2. **Scoop** out the insides, then fill each tiny tomato with cheese. **pop** the lids back on.

The Captain's Table

Pirate peppers

X marks the spot!

Dive-in dips

Guacamole and sour cream chips

Fish snack
with vegetables

Make it snappy!

Fine food for hungry sailors!

Tomato and cheese balls

Cheesy bread map

Skull and crossbones

Index